Ghostly Warnings

Ghostly Warnings

DANIEL COHEN

Illustrated by
DAVID LINN

COBBLEHILL BOOKS

Dutton   New York

Library of Congress Cataloging-in-Publication Data
Cohen, Daniel, date
Ghostly warnings / Daniel Cohen : illustrated by David Linn.
p.   cm.
Summary: A collection of stories from beyond the grave in which
ghosts or spirits spell out the impending doom of the person warned.
ISBN 0-525-65227-2
1. Ghosts.   2. Parapsychology.   [1. Ghosts.   2. Parapsychology.]
I. Linn, David, ill.   II. Title.
BF1461.C6683   1996   133.1—dc20   96-17111   CIP   AC

Published in the United States by Cobblehill Books,
an affiliate of Dutton Children's Books,
a division of Penguin Books USA Inc.
375 Hudson Street, New York, New York 10014

Printed in the United States of America
First Edition 10 9 8 7 6 5 4 3 2 1

Contents

The Fetch

Of all the warnings of death, it is the spirit the British call "the fetch," or co-walker, that is the most terrifying. It is the most terrifying because it is the most familiar. It is you!

Here is a story about "the fetch" that has been told for over three hundred years.

Most of the family had left on a short visit. Mary did

not go along with the rest. She did not feel strong enough for the trip, brief as it was. She had been seriously ill for many months. Just last week the doctor had pronounced her vastly improved and out of danger. This was a great relief to the young woman and her family. But still she did not really have her strength back.

Mary walked slowly through the garden of the large house. After spending so much time in bed, she was now able to enjoy the sights and scents of a late English spring. Her delight in the simple act of being able to walk through a garden was keener than ever.

As she passed close to the house, Mary glanced up. She thought she saw a face at one of the second-floor windows. She couldn't make out the features of the face, and in an instant it disappeared. But she had the distinct impression that it was a woman who was staring intently at her from the window. One of the servants, Mary thought. Yet somehow the sight of that face at the window made her uncomfortable. It was a familiar face, but she couldn't quite recognize it.

Mary took one more turn around the garden. Then she began to feel very tired. "After all," she told herself,

"I have only been out of bed for a few days. Being tired is natural." Still, she decided that it was time to go back inside the house.

Once inside, the young woman was gripped by the indefinable but very definite feeling that something was wrong. At first, she couldn't put her finger on what was amiss. Then she realized that the house was so quiet. It was much too quiet. Yes, her family was gone, but there should be some servants around. What about that woman she had seen at the second-floor window?

There was also the feeling of being watched. Mary didn't see anyone. She certainly didn't hear anyone. But, nonetheless, the feeling that she was being watched was very strong.

Mary went into the main hall and started to climb the great staircase to the second floor. Then she did hear a sound, a gentle rustling of what might have been a woman's skirt. The sound was faint and, under normal circumstances, would have passed unnoticed. But in the unnatural quiet of the house, the sound was startling.

Mary looked up quickly and thought that she saw the hem of a skirt in the shadows on the second-floor landing. But as soon as she saw it, the vision faded into the darkness. Mary wasn't really sure that she had seen anything at all.

Feeling more uneasy than ever, and quite shaken, Mary entered her own room. She went to the mirror and inspected her face. Earlier in the day her cheeks had been rosy, and she had looked very nearly her old self again. Now her face was drawn and pale. She looked very ill.

And then she saw something else in the mirror. There was a figure standing behind her. It had not come in through the door. It had simply appeared.

At first, the face was indistinct. Mary could only see that it was a woman's face. She heard the sound of a skirt rustling behind her. The figure was moving toward her, but she was now too afraid to turn around. The figure came closer. It was looking directly at Mary's image in the mirror.

It took a moment for Mary to recognize the second figure in the mirror. But the face was certainly a familiar one. It was Mary's own face. The second figure was her own exact double—but the double was not breathing,

and when it opened its lips to speak, there was no sound.

Mary had seen "the fetch," and she knew what that meant. If you see your double, it means you are about to die.

A few hours later the family returned. They found Mary on the bed, feverish, hysterical, and clearly dying. She managed to gasp out an account of what had happened. Within an hour she was dead.

Deadly Doubles and
Second Chances

Tales of the deadly warning double come from all over the world. Perhaps the most famous story of a double concerns the French writer Guy de Maupassant.

In 1885, de Maupassant was at work in his study one evening when a figure appeared at the door, walked across the room, and sat down in front of him. The figure then began dictating to de Maupassant the words of the story that he was working on.

The writer was astounded. How could this person have gotten into his study? How could he know the very words that he intended to write? Who was he? It was then that de Maupassant realized, to his horror, that the man sitting across from him was no stranger, but his exact double.

The figure soon vanished, but the incident left de Maupassant a badly shaken man. This figure was the first warning of a disease that was soon to overtake the writer and lead to his insanity and death.

The English poet Percy Bysshe Shelley was living in Italy and attended the popular carnival in Venice. As he made his way through the streets crowded with masked and costumed revelers, he noticed that one figure seemed to be following him. It was a man in a long black cloak, whose face was shrouded by a hood.

The poet finally became annoyed. He stopped and turned to the figure that was now standing right behind him. "Who are you? What do you want?" he shouted. The figure pulled back the hood, revealing his face—

which was Shelley's own face. Then he said chillingly, "Now are you satisfied?"

The next year the boat on which the poet was a passenger went down in a storm and he was drowned.

Meeting one's double is not always an omen of death or ill fortune. The great German writer Goethe was riding down a path to the town of Drusenheim when:

"I saw myself on horseback coming toward me on the same path, dressed in a suit such as I had never worn, pale grey with some gold." In a moment the figure vanished.

But, Goethe continued, "I found myself returned on the same path eight years afterward . . . and then I wore the suit I had worn in the vision. And I had not worn that suit deliberately, but by chance."

A California artist named Catherine Reinhart said that she saw her double on a number of occasions. Usually the figure looked about five years older than she did at the moment she saw it.

The most striking experience came when she was

twenty-eight. She saw her double at a party. The double looked a little older, and walked with a slight limp. Four years later, Catherine Reinhart was in a serious auto accident. Her husband was killed and her leg was badly injured. She never fully recovered from the accident and walked with a slight limp for the rest of her life.

There are even a few cases in which the double's warning is supposed to have saved a person's life. Alex B. Griffith believed that his double saved his life—twice.

The first time was in the summer of 1944, during World War II. Griffith was an infantry sergeant leading a patrol in France. There was no sign of danger, and Griffith and his men felt quite safe.

Then Griffith saw a figure on the road ahead. The figure was his double, and it was waving its arms and appeared to be shouting, though no words could be heard. The figure was obviously trying to make Sergeant Griffith and his men stop. But no one aside from Griffith could see the figure. The men were surprised and puzzled when their sergeant abruptly ordered them to turn back. He didn't explain why. He couldn't. He just knew that if they went any farther down that road they would be killed.

As he sat on the ground trying to figure out what to do next, Griffith saw an American supply vehicle pass and head down the road to the spot where he had seen the double. There was a sudden burst of machine-gun fire, and the vehicle went wildly out of control. Its driver had been killed in the volley. Somewhere up ahead a German machine gun was hidden to guard the road. If Sergeant Griffith and his men had gone any farther, they would have been gunned down, just as the vehicle had been.

Twenty years later, Griffith saw the double again. It wasn't Griffith as he was in 1964, but Sergeant Griffith as he had been in 1944. Griffith and his family were out on a hike in the woods. There had been a tremendous storm the night before, and the winds were still gusty.

The little group rounded a bend in the trail, and there was the figure of the young Sergeant Griffith in uniform, waving its arms and shouting wordlessly, just as it had done on the road in France. As before, no one else saw the figure, but Griffith knew what the warning meant.

He instantly told his family to stop and turn back.

A few seconds later a huge tree, weakened by the storm, came crashing down into a clearing where Griffith and his family would have been had it not been for the warning.

The White Lady of Berlin

Throughout history there are tales of families plagued by a warning ghost or spirit. The apparition, which is said to appear when a member of the family is about to die, or when some other calamity is about to happen, can take many forms. For the powerful Hohenzollern family, rulers of the German state of Prussia, the warning spirit came in the form of a lady dressed all in white.

No one knew the origins of the White Lady. There

was much speculation as to who she might have been in life. All that was known for certain was that for centuries she had been seen from time to time in the corridors of the Old Palace in Berlin. Her appearance usually was followed by some death or disaster for the ruling family.

The legend goes back a long way, but the first recorded appearance of the White Lady was in 1619, during the reign of John Sigismund. A page was walking down a corridor in the Old Palace when he came face-to-face with the figure of a woman dressed in white gliding silently toward him. The figure was holding a white veil in front of her face. The page had heard rumors of the ghost, but refused to be frightened by it. He stood in the ghost's path, put his hand on her arm, and asked, "Where might you be going, madam?"

The White Lady drew a hand from behind her veil. In it she held the great key—the key that was said to unlock all of the castle's six hundred doors. She brought the key heavily down on the page's head. He fell to the ground dead.

Just as this happened, two fellow servants came

around the corner. They had more sense than the dead boy. They stood back as the White Lady flitted past.

On the next day, John Sigismund died suddenly.

The most curious story about the White Lady involved Frederick the Great, the most famous of all the Hohenzollern rulers. Frederick was known to be a man who did not believe in anything supernatural. He certainly did not believe in ghosts. And the White Lady was never reported to have appeared during his long and successful reign.

Yet after death, Frederick the Great's attitude toward ghosts may have changed. Here is what happened. When his nephew, Frederick William II, invaded France, he first met with great success. His armies reached all the way to the outskirts of Paris.

Frederick William himself was staying at the French city of Verdun. One evening he was dissatisfied with the wine that had been brought to him for dinner. He went down into the wine cellar in search of something better. There, amid the bottles and barrels, stood the ghost of his uncle, Frederick the Great.

"Unless you call off the Prussian army from Paris,

nephew," said the ghost, "you may expect to see some-one who will not be welcome to you."

The terrified Frederick William said that he did not know what his uncle's ghost meant.

"I mean," replied Frederick the Great, "the White Lady of the Old Palace, and I am sure you know what *her* visit implies." And then the spirit faded away.

Frederick William took the warning very seriously. He called off his troops, returned to Berlin, and lived for another five years.

The White Lady appeared just before a battle in which Prince Louis of Prussia was killed by Napoleon's army.

She appeared once again in June, 1914. The death that followed was not that of Kaiser William II, but the assassination of his relative, the Archduke Francis Ferdinand, heir to the throne of Austria. This killing led to World War I, and ultimately to the total destruction of the old Prussian monarchy.

After the war, the Old Palace was turned first into a government office building and later into a museum. The White Lady was never seen again.

The Murderous Husband

There are many ways in which people have believed that they are able to communicate with the spirits, or "the other side." One of them is by what is called "automatic writing." A spirit is supposed to seize control of a person's hand and force them to write out a message. Often it is a message that the writer does not understand.

Another method that is used is a device called the Ouija board. It is a smooth and highly polished board with letters and numbers on it. Two people will sit with the board between them, their fingers resting lightly on a small teardrop-shaped, tablelike object. This is called the *planchette*. The planchette moves easily over the board. The spirits are supposed to guide it to spell out a message or the answer to a question.

Both of these methods were used in the warning sent to a Michigan woman named Celeste McVoy Holden.

She had recently separated from her husband. She and her four-month-old daughter were spending the summer in a large house on the northern shore of Lake Michigan near the resort town of Pentwater.

Celeste had a chauffeur and a maid. But they were local people who were at the house during the day and returned to their homes in the nearby town at night. At night Celeste and the baby were alone. And it was very lonely in the rambling and isolated house.

Celeste invited her friend, Buell Mullen, and her husband to spend a few weeks at the lakeshore house. Buell came first. Her husband had some business to attend to and promised to join her in a few days.

Shortly after she arrived, Buell went to her room to

write her husband a letter. She wanted to give him exact directions to the isolated house. But when she sat down to write, it was as if some unseen force had taken control of her hand.

She watched as her hand began to scrawl a message across the paper without any conscious control on her part. The handwriting was totally unlike her own writing. The message was simple and ominous: "Beware! Beware! Beware!"

"Beware of what?" thought Buell. And then her hand scrawled one more word across the paper: "Jack."

Buell Mullen ran to Celeste Holden's room with the message. Celeste turned white when she saw it. Jack was the name of her former husband. One of the reasons that she left him was that he had a violent temper. Was this some sort of warning that he planned to harm the women?

Both women knew about Ouija boards, which were extremely popular at that time. They went into town and were able to buy one. Back home, they sat with the board across their knees, their fingers resting on the planchette.

Celeste asked what was going to happen. The board quickly spelled out a terrifying answer: "Murder, you and your child. Prepare."

How could they prepare? They were alone. They were unarmed. First, Celeste called the chauffeur at his home. She didn't tell him what she was afraid of, but asked him if he could come back at a moment's notice. He said that he could.

Then they got ready for the night by locking every door, and securing every window in the large house. They took the baby and went into what they thought was the most secure room in the house. They piled furniture against the doors and blocked the windows of the room.

Then they waited. The two women were not able to sleep. They sat and played cards all through the night. Every time there was a sound, and there are many unexplained sounds in an old house, they stopped and listened.

Eventually morning came. As the sky began to lighten, Celeste and Buell began to feel a little silly. Nothing had happened. They were happy about that. But had they taken the whole business with the message and the

Ouija board too seriously? They thought they had, and they didn't tell anybody how they had spent the night in fear.

Then, two days later a friend of the family called to ask Celeste if she had seen her former husband, Jack. Celeste was startled. She said no, that she assumed he was back in the city where he worked.

Then the friend told her that two nights before, Jack had turned up in Pentwater. He had walked into a party very drunk, and acting crazy. He was waving a gun and saying that he was going to kill his ex-wife and baby.

Some of the other guests had managed to wrestle the gun away from Jack, and calmed him down. He left the party at about three in the morning, and no one had seen him since. The friend assumed that Jack had left town.

Had Jack actually calmed down and left town? Or had he come to the house sometime that night with the intention of killing his wife and daughter? Perhaps he was turned away by the locked and barricaded doors?

In any event, the warning from "the other side" was a timely one.

The Black Velvet Ribbon

The story of Lady Beresford and the black velvet ribbon that she wore around her wrist has been handed down in the Beresford family since the eighteenth century.

Lady Beresford and her brother, Lord Tyrone, were born in Ireland. They were orphaned while they were still young. When they were growing up, they relied on one another and became very close. They made a solemn pact. Whichever one of them should die first would, if

31

possible, appear to the other after death. Even after Lady Beresford married, she continued to see a great deal of her brother.

One morning she came down to breakfast looking very pale and drawn. Clearly she had spent a sleepless night. Her husband asked if she were ill, but she insisted that she was quite well.

"Have you hurt your wrist?" he asked, for he noticed that her wrist was now bound by a black ribbon.

She said that nothing had happened. Then, after a moment, she continued. "Let me beg of you, sir, never to ask about this ribbon again. From this day forward, you will not see me without it. If it concerned you as a husband, I would tell you at once. I have never refused you any request, but about this ribbon I can say nothing. I beg that you never bring the subject up again."

Her husband was puzzled, even alarmed. But if that was what Lady Beresford wanted so strongly, he felt he had no choice but to agree.

For the rest of breakfast, Lady Beresford was very nervous. She asked the servant if the morning mail had arrived, but was told that it had not. A few moments later, she rang the bell and once again asked the servant about the mail. Once again she was told that it had not arrived yet.

"Do you expect any letters," her husband asked, "that you are so anxious about the arrival of the mail?"

"I do," she answered. "I expect to hear that Lord Tyrone is dead, that he died last Tuesday at four o'clock."

Her husband was astonished. He had never known his wife to be superstitious or prey to gloomy thoughts of death. He assumed that she must have had some sort of bad dream or nightmare that upset her. But at that moment the servant entered and handed Lady Beresford a letter sealed in black. She opened it and glanced at the contents. "It is as I expected," she said. "He is dead."

Her husband looked at the letter. It contained the news of Lord Tyrone's death—on the previous Tuesday at four o'clock, just as his wife had said.

Lady Beresford had another bit of news for her husband. "I can assure you without the possibility of doubt that I am going to have a baby and the child will be a boy." The couple already had two daughters and had longed for a son.

Some seven months after she made her announcement, Lady Beresford did indeed have a boy. The couple's joy, however, was short-lived. Just a few years later, Lord Beresford died.

After her husband's death, the widow's way of life changed completely. She moved out of the family estate into a small house, and rarely left it. As far as the world at large was concerned, she became a recluse. Her only company was a clergyman, his wife, and young son. She lived this way for several years. Then one day she astonished and shocked her neighbors by marrying the clergyman's son, despite the great differences in their ages and social position.

The marriage was a disaster almost from the start. The young man turned out to be the opposite of his pious father. He was a terrible person, and after several years she separated from him. When that happened, he appeared to be very sorry for the way he had acted, insisted he had changed, and pleaded that she take him back. She did, but found that he was no different than before.

One day Lady Beresford invited a few friends over for a visit. One was an elderly clergyman from Ireland, who had known her family for a long time.

Lady Beresford seemed to be in exceptionally good spirits. She said, "It is my birthday. I am forty-eight today."

"No, my lady," said the clergyman, "you are mistaken. Your family and I had many disputes about your age, and recently I was in the parish where you were born. I searched the register and find that you are only forty-seven today."

The clergyman assumed that Lady Beresford would be happy to discover that she was a year younger than she had believed. Her reaction, however, was quite the reverse. She turned deathly pale, and gasped. "You have signed my death warrant." She then excused herself from her guests, saying that she had some important arrangements to make and she had not much longer to live.

She called for her son, then about twelve years old, and her closest friend, Lady Betty Cobb. She said that she had something to tell them.

Lady Beresford started by reminding them of her brother, Lord Tyrone, and the pledge to return after death that the brother and sister had made. One night, many years ago, she awoke to find the ghost of Lord Tyrone standing at her bedside.

"Have you forgotten our promise?" the ghost said. "I died last Tuesday at four o'clock."

The specter of Lord Tyrone told his sister that she would soon have a son. Then he said that her husband would die within a few years, but that she would marry again and her second husband would make her miserable. "And you will die in the forty-seventh year of your age," he concluded.

Lady Beresford was horrified by the future that was laid out for her by the ghost. She said, "When morning comes, I shall believe that all of this was just a dream."

"Will not the news of my death convince you otherwise?"

"No. I might have had such a dream that accidentally came true. I will need stronger proof."

"I can give you proof, but it will injure you irreparably."

"I do not mind."

"You are a woman of courage," the phantom said. "Hold out your hand."

"He then touched my wrist with a hand that was as cold as marble. In an instant all of the nerves and sinews were shrunken. 'Now,' he said, 'let no one see your wrist while you live.' Then the phantom was gone. In the morning I found a piece of black ribbon and bound up my wrist."

Events proceeded exactly as Lord Tyrone had foretold. After the death of her husband, Lady Beresford tried to escape her fate by living in seclusion, seeing only a clergyman and his family. "Little did I imagine that their son, a mere youth, was the person destined by Fate to prove my undoing.

"I believed that I had been able to escape Fate, because I thought I had passed my forty-seventh birthday.

But today I heard that I am mistaken about my age and I am now only forty-seven. I therefore have no doubt that my death is at hand."

She said that once she was dead the need to conceal her wrist was over. She asked Lady Betty to take the ribbon from her wrist, "so that you and my son may witness the truth of what I have related."

Lady Beresford died before midnight. Lady Betty ordered the servants to leave the room. Then she and the boy untied the ribbon that the dead woman had worn about her wrist for so many years. They found the wrist exactly as she had described it, with every nerve and sinew shrunk.

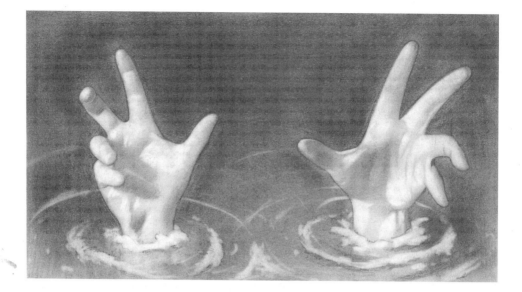

A Living Ghost

Is it possible for a person to see the "ghost" of someone not yet dead? Is such an apparition really a ghost? That's a matter of opinion. However, there are many cases in which individuals are reported to have foreseen the death of another. Here is a striking case that took place about one hundred years ago.

A man named Jones was taking a long walk by the river. He became tired and sat down to rest on the river bank. At first, he felt calm and peaceful. But then, for some reason he could not understand, Jones became nervous and frightened.

He tried to leave, but found he couldn't get up. Then what appeared to be a black cloud or fog rose up in front of him. In the middle of the cloud he saw a man in a brown suit. Suddenly, the man in the brown suit jumped into the water and sank from sight.

Jones was horrified by the sight. After a few minutes the shock began to wear off. The fog disappeared, and he found he was able to move again. There had been no man in a brown suit. The whole thing had been some sort of a waking dream, an hallucination. Nothing had really happened except in Jones's mind.

Still, Jones was very upset by what he had experienced. When he got home, he described the incident to his sister in great detail. She told him to forget it. She said it was morbid to dwell on such a subject. She said he must have fallen asleep by the river and just had a bad dream.

Jones agreed that it probably was just a dream, and he did try to forget the experience. But he couldn't.

The image of the man in the brown suit jumping into the water was just too solid, too powerful for him to forget.

The very next week a man named Espie drowned himself in the river at the very spot where Jones had seen his vision of the man in the brown suit. Espie had been wearing a brown suit at the time of his death. An account of Espie's death appeared in the newspaper where Jones read it.

In a suicide note, Espie said that he was very depressed and had been thinking about killing himself for a long time. But Jones had never met Espie. Until he read about the suicide in the newspaper, Jones had never heard of the man. He had no way of knowing what Espie planned to do, because he had never known Espie.

What happened? Was it simply a coincidence? Was Jones somehow able to read Espie's thoughts? Did Jones have a vision of the future? Or had he seen a ghost-to-be?

You decide.

The River Ghost

On September 8, 1777, the Reverend James Crawford went out for a ride. Seated behind him on his horse was his sister-in-law, Hannah Wilson.

There had been a good deal of rain during the previous week, and the river was high. When they came to the river's edge, Miss Wilson became concerned. She thought the river, which was usually very low and easy to cross at this spot, now looked dangerous. She was afraid that the current was too swift, that the horse might lose its footing, and they could be swept away if they tried to cross.

The Reverend Mr. Crawford, however, had a different opinion. "I do not think that there can be any danger," he said. "I see another horseman crossing just twenty yards in front of us." Miss Wilson also saw the second horseman. The Reverend Mr. Crawford called out to the rider to ask if there was any danger.

The rider stopped and turned around. As he did so, Rev. Crawford and Miss Wilson realized that the face that looked back at them was no longer human. The face of the rider was ghostly white and almost glowed with hate and evil.

The Reverend Mr. Crawford was astonished and terrified by the sight. Miss Wilson was just as terrified. She began screaming and couldn't stop. Rev. Crawford turned his horse around and rode back home as quickly as he could.

Rev. Crawford was a relative newcomer to the area. When he told of his experience, he was surprised to discover that the local people had heard the story before.

They told him that the spirit of the terrible ghostly rider appeared at the river just before someone was about to drown. Everyone seemed to have a different idea of who the ghostly rider was, and why he haunted the river. But one thing they were all sure of was that someone was about to be drowned when he appeared.

This belief in ghosts bothered the Reverend Mr. Crawford. He assumed that there was some perfectly natural explanation for the rider—though he had to admit that the terrible face had frightened him badly. Still, he could not let people think that he was so superstitious and foolish as to believe in warning spirits. No one in the neighborhood would have any respect for him as a minister.

So, on September 27, he determined once again to ride across the river. He had no particular reason to go across the river. He just wanted to show people, and perhaps prove to himself, that he was not superstitious.

Just exactly what happened, no one knows. Crossing the river should have been quite safe. But a few hours after Rev. Crawford set out on his journey, his riderless horse returned home. Crawford's body was found just downstream from the place where he would have crossed the river. Apparently, he had been drowned.

By September 27, the water in the river was again quite low, and how the Reverend Mr. Crawford had been drowned in what was little more than a trickle of water remains a mystery. Was the ghostly rider a warning of his death?

"Forever!"

Missouri farmer Henry Burchard and his wife, Harriet, were inseparable. Too inseparable, as it turned out.

Harriet was a jealous woman. She always insisted that Henry was "too handsome for his own good." In order to keep him from straying toward women who were younger and prettier than she was, Harriet simply stuck to Henry. Wherever he went, she was there watching him.

If her distrust annoyed Henry, he never said anything about it. Every once in a while he might comment that Harriet "must have been born jealous." But it was a mild complaint, and he never gave her any real cause for concern.

In the winter of 1873, Harriet Burchard died of consumption. She and Henry had just celebrated their thirteenth wedding anniversary. Henry was genuinely saddened by his wife's death. Despite her jealousy, she had been a good wife, and he missed her terribly.

But Henry Burchad was still a young man, and now he was a very lonely one. He remembered that Harriet had always told him, "Man was not meant to live alone."

No one in the small farming community of Kirksville was surprised or shocked when, in the spring after Harriet's death, Henry Burchard married Catherine Webster, a young widow. Catherine's husband had been killed in a farming accident some years earlier. Catherine had known both Henry and Harriet.

About three weeks after her marriage to Henry, Catherine was home alone when a tremendous crash shook the house. It sounded as if a shower of rocks had come

clattering across the roof. When Catherine went outside, she found rocks scattered all around the house. But who had thrown them? There was no one around. The nearest neighbor was half a mile away.

As she stood wondering what had happened, Catherine saw the rocks rise up off the ground, hover above the house, and drop back down on the roof. At this sight, the poor woman was nearly paralyzed with fear.

When Henry returned home from town that evening, Catherine tried to explain to him what had happened. But he didn't take the story seriously. He thought she was just tired and overwrought from the recent wedding.

The next night, while the couple slept, their bedclothes were snatched away. Henry, shivering in the cold, jumped out of bed to see what had happened. The bedclothes were heaped on the floor. He wondered if a breeze had blown them off. But the windows were all closed. Had Catherine been restless and pulled them off by accident? She appeared to be sleeping peacefully.

Henry was puzzled, but tired. He put the covers back on the bed, and drifted back to sleep. And then it happened again. Catherine was still asleep, but he wondered if she were faking. Perhaps she was trying to get back at him for not taking her story about the rocks seriously.

When he remade the bed this time, he tucked the covers in as tightly as possible. It was going to take a real effort to get them off now.

After some time, Henry got back to sleep again. And as soon as he did, the pillow was pulled out from under his head. He found it on the floor. He decided that Catherine must be responsible. She was still sleeping peacefully, but she was the only other person in the room.

He got up and lit the lantern. He was just in time to see the pillow fly out from under the head of the sleeping Catherine and fall down at his feet. Her head fell back against the mattress and she woke up screaming.

Henry didn't want to frighten her. "You were restless," he said. "I thought maybe you were having a nightmare. You threw your pillow on the floor." He handed it back to her.

Catherine said that she didn't remember anything.

"No," he said. "But it's very late now and we both need sleep." He tucked the covers in tightly, put out the lantern, and went back to bed. Nothing else happened that night.

But the same mysterious events occurred the next night, and the next. Catherine seemed able to sleep on. But Henry was awake half the night worrying and watching.

He found it increasingly difficult to sleep at all. He took to sitting up and reading by the dim lamplight until very late. One night as he started to get into bed, the covers were rolled back as if by an invisible hand. There was a message written on the underside of the white coverlet.

Henry recognized the handwriting as that of Harriet, his first wife. The message read: "These things shall continue forever!"

A Warning of Plague

In the winter of 1665, an English clergyman named John Rudell wrote in his diary of a very strange experience. Rudell was curate in the parish of South Petherwin in Cornwall. One bleak January day he was called to the home of one of his parishioners, a man named Bligh.

Bligh was very upset. But at first he seemed unwilling to say why. The two men took a private walk across the fields, and Bligh began to talk. He said that his son, a boy of about thirteen, was being haunted.

Each morning as the boy went off to school, he had to cross a meadow near his house. As he crossed the meadow, the boy was approached by a ghost. Bligh described the ghost as that of a pale, sad-looking young woman. The figure did not walk, but floated a few inches above the ground.

The ghost did not in any way threaten the boy. But it stared at him intently. The boy was badly frightened, and didn't want to cross the meadow anymore.

Bligh was at first inclined to dismiss the story as a product of the boy's overactive imagination. But his son was able to supply more details about the appearance of the apparition. Then Bligh realized that what the boy saw was the ghost of a woman named Dorothy Dinglet. She had been a friend of the Bligh family who had died three years before.

John Rudell was also inclined to take the matter seriously. He suggested that the next day they should accompany the boy to the meadow and see if the ghost appeared to all of them.

At dawn, the two men and the boy began to cross the meadow. The boy's small dog trotted alongside them. At first, everything seemed quite ordinary. Then, at the corner of the meadow, they noticed a faint bright shape appear and begin to drift toward them. As it came closer, the shape took a human form. Both men recognized the ghost of Dorothy Dinglet shimmering in the early morning light.

The ghost stared directly at the curate. He was frightened, but he addressed it, and asked it to speak, "to prove it was not a fiend." In a soft voice, the spirit uttered a single, terrible sentence: "Before next Yuletide, a fearful pestilence will lay waste the land, and many souls will be loosed from their flesh." The men shivered, and the dog whined. The ghostly figure then disappeared.

Rudell was convinced that what he and the others had seen truly was the ghost of Dorothy Dinglet, and not some diabolical trick. He did not know why the ghost walked the earth. Was it only to deliver her warning of what was to come? He performed a ceremony which would allow the troubled soul of the young woman to rest peacefully.

The curate remembered the ghost's prophecy. In June of that year, England was struck by a heat wave. This appeared to be the event that triggered the outbreak of the great plague of London. So many died that no one was left to bury them and bodies rotted in the streets.

During the summer the disease spread from the city into the countryside. It decimated the land until winter, when the cold killed the rats which carried the plague germs. By Christmastime, seventy thousand people had died. It was the last major epidemic of plague to strike England, and it was by far the worst.

The ghost had been right. "A fearful pestilence" had indeed laid waste to the land.

No Escape

A common thread that runs through many tales of ghostly warnings is that the warnings do no good; that there is no way to escape Fate. Here are two classic tales which illustrate that point.

The first comes from eighteenth-century England. It concerns Lord Lyttleton, one of a long line of distinguished men who had that title. This particular Lord Lyttleton, however, was not particularly distinguished.

In fact, he was known as "the bad" Lord Lyttleton.

During the night of November 24, 1779, Lord Lyttleton was awakened by what sounded like a bird fluttering near his bed. But when he opened his eyes, he found that it was no bird. He saw standing by the bed the figure of a woman that he had wronged and abandoned many years earlier and who, "when deserted, had put a violent end to her own existence."

The ghost pointed to a clock that was just visible in the half-light. Then it announced that in three days, to the minute, Lord Lyttleton would be dead.

Lord Lyttleton was badly shaken by the experience. He tried to pass it off lightly, and even made jokes about it to his friends. He insisted that he was going to "bilk the ghost." But he was not really able to hide his fear.

On the third, and fatal night, Lord Lyttleton was so upset that his friends were really worried about him. In order to try and calm him down, they secretly advanced all the clocks in the house by one hour. The result was that when the fatal hour apparently came and went, Lord Lyttleton was completely unaffected.

Thus, he went to bed feeling more cheerful than he

had in days. Before going to sleep, Lord Lyttleton was chatting with his valet. The servant left the room, and then a church clock nearby struck the real time. The servant heard a loud choking sound coming from the bedroom, and when he rushed back, he found that his master had suddenly and violently choked to death for no apparent reason.

In some Middle Eastern countries, there is a belief that Death appears in the form of a tall woman dressed all in black. According to one story, there was a servant who was purchasing food for his master's household in the Baghdad market one afternoon. The servant saw the figure of Death standing nearby. She looked directly at him and appeared to make a threatening gesture.

The servant was terrified. He ran to his master's house and told him what had happened. He then asked his master for a loan of a horse. He wanted to flee to the city of Samarra, where Death would not find him.

The master agreed, and the servant immediately rode off as fast as he could. He expected to reach Samarra before nightfall.

The master himself then went to the marketplace to see if Death would appear.

She was there. She walked without hurrying among the stands. From time to time she would tap a person on the shoulder. When that happened, the person turned pale and hurried away.

The merchant walked up to Death, and asked her why she had threatened his servant.

"He was mistaken," Death said quietly. "That was not a threatening gesture. It was only a gesture of surprise. I did not expect to see him here in Baghdad. I have an appointment with him tonight in Samarra, you see."

She smiled and disappeared.